I CAN READ Books®
by Crosby Bonsall

An I Can Read Book®

The Case of the
Scaredy Cats

by CROSBY BONSALL

HarperCollins*Publishers*

Library of Congress Catalog Card Number: 75–159039
ISBN 0–06–020565–2
ISBN 0–06–020566–0 (lib. bdg.)
ISBN 0–06–444047–8 (pbk.)

10 11 12 13 SCP 20 19

for Edith Ten Broeck Bonsall

"Girls!" Snitch yelled.

"A broom!" cried Wizard.

"A flower pot!" said Tubby.

"A snowlady!" said Skinny.

7

"I told you

old Marigold and her gang

moved in," Snitch said.

But the clubhouse was not for girls.

The sign on the door said so.

The clubhouse was for private eyes.

The sign on the door said so.

Wizard and his brother Snitch,

and their friends Skinny and Tubby

were private eyes.

Wizard was their leader.

The sign on the door said so.

Snitch said, "Can't they read?"

Marigold came out.

She said, "Let us join your club

or you stay out."

Then she slammed the door. Hard.

"How do we get them out?

We can't hit them," Skinny said.

"Why not?" Snitch wanted to know.

"They're girls," Tubby told him.

"Six of them," Skinny said.

"And they are big," Snitch cried.

"So what," Wizard said.

"Girls are girls.

Come on. I have a plan."

First the boys went to the store.

The grocer gave them

some empty boxes.

They took them to Tubby's house.

"Girls are silly," Wizard said.

"They cry a lot."

Then he told the boys his plan.

They used Tubby's paints,

and rope, and the boxes.

"It will be easy," Wizard said.

"No fighting. No yelling.

When the girls see us

they will run away for good."

That made the boys smile.

But Gussie and Gertie did not smile

when they saw Snitch's sign.

"Don't even look," Marigold said.

Nobody smiled at Tubby's sign.

Not Alice. Not Annie.

"What does it say?" Annie asked.

"Never mind," Marigold said.

"Don't even look."

And Millie did not smile

at Skinny's sign.

"Don't even look," Marigold said.

But when Marigold

saw Wizard's sign about her,

she forgot everything she had told

Gussie and Gertie and Alice

and Annie and Millie.

Marigold tackled Wizard.

And there was plenty of fighting,

and plenty of yelling.

Alice grabbed Tubby,

and Annie helped.

Gussie and Gertie

tied up Snitch.

23

And Millie

pushed Skinny.

24

Tubby got Annie's thumb

out of his ear.

He ran to hide

behind the garbage can.

Skinny ran to hide

up a tree.

Snitch ran to hide

behind the garbage can

with Tubby.

And Wizard ran to hide

on the roof.

"Well," said Marigold,

"we took care of those boys.

All of them. And--"

She looked around.

"Where is Annie?" she cried.

Annie was not there.

"How can I tell Annie's mother

we lost her?" Marigold cried.

Alice started to cry.

"She was my best friend," she said.

"I'll miss her," sobbed Gertie.

"I liked her," cried Gussie.

"So did I," wailed Millie.

The girls cried so loud

the boys heard them.

They ran from their hiding places.

"I told you they cry a lot,"

Wizard said.

"What is the matter now?"

Wizard asked.

"We lost a girl," Marigold cried.

"That," said Wizard,

"is a case for private eyes.

We are just the ones you need."

"Give us the girl's name,

please," Wizard said.

"It's Annie," Marigold told him.

"What does she look like?"

Skinny asked.

"It's Annie!" Marigold yelled.

"You know Annie.

Annie is your sister."

"When was she last seen?"

Tubby asked.

"You just got her thumb

out of your ear

a minute ago," Marigold cried.

"Did you look for Annie?"
Wizard asked.

Marigold said, "No."

"Boy, do you need us!" Wizard said.

"I will look in the clubhouse,

my men will look around,

and you girls can cry."

Annie was not

in the clubhouse.

But Wizard found

one hair ribbon

and a string of beads.

Annie was not anywhere.

They called and called for her.

"Does Annie hear okay?" Wizard asked.

"Sure," Skinny said.

"There is only one thing

wrong with Annie.

She is a scaredy cat."

40

"She wasn't scared to put her thumb
in my ear," Tubby said.

"She can run faster than you,"
Skinny told him.

"Anyway," Tubby said,

"Annie always gave me her lollipop

while she sucked her thumb."

"She was nice," Snitch said.

"Not bad for a girl," Wizard said.

"We will have to find her,"

said Skinny.

"It will make Mom happy."

AH-CHOO!

"Who sneezed?" Wizard asked.

"I didn't," Marigold said.

"Did you, Millie?"

"No. Did you, Gussie?"

"No. Did you, Gertie?"

"No. Did you, Alice?"

"No. Did you, Snitch?"

"No. Did you, Tub?"

"No. Did you, Skin?"

"No. Did you, Wiz?"

"I ASKED THE QUESTION,"
Wizard said.

"Oh."

"That sign is sneezing,"

Snitch yelled.

"What sign?" Wizard cried.

"The sign with the mittens,"

Snitch yelled.

"Oh," said Wizard.

"Signs do not sneeze,"

Wizard told Snitch.

Then he yelled,

"The sign with the *mittens*!"

"Everybody stay back!" Tubby cried.

"It may not be safe."

One by one,

they all got behind Wizard.

Slowly...slowly...slowly

they sneaked up on the sign.

51

"Those are Annie's mittens,"

Wizard whispered.

"That is Annie's hat,"

Marigold whispered.

"Are they on Annie?" Snitch asked.

"Annie, are you in there?"

Wizard yelled.

"Now don't be scared.

There is nothing

to be scared about."

It was Annie.

"I'm scared of YOU,"

she yelled back.

"You boys scared me.

You ran away and hid."

"Us? Run?" Wizard said.

"You ran and hid

on the roof," Annie said.

"I was fixing a leak," Wizard said.

"Skinny ran and hid

in a tree," Annie said.

"I was looking for apples,"

Skinny said.

"Tubby and Snitch ran and hid

behind the garbage can," Annie said.

"I was looking for cookies,"
Tubby said.

"I was helping him look,"
Snitch said.

"They looked scared to me,"

Annie said. "So I hid, too."

"They *were* scared," Marigold said.

"Scared of girls.

They were running away from us."

"Scared of me?" Annie said.

"Running away from me?"

"Yes," said Marigold.

"Wait till I tell Mama," Annie said.

59

"You can stop being scared now,"

Marigold told the boys.

"We are taking Annie home.

It is going to snow."

"You see?" Wizard said.

"I told you the girls would run away.

I hope they never come back."

Hurray!

The girls were gone.

The case was solved.

And it was snowing!

Everything

was just the same.

63

Well, almost the same.